Little Red Riding Hood and the Dragon

Written by
Ying Chang
Compestine

Illustrated by
Joy Ang

Abrams Books for Young Readers
New York

By now, you have probably heard the old folk tale about a girl in a red cape. She and her grandmother were gobbled up by a wolf but were rescued by a woodsman.

The truth is that the tale took place here in China, there wasn't a woodsman, and I, the gentle wolf, certainly was not the one who ate them.

Here is the *real* story.

ONCE UPON A TIME, there lived a
little girl in a village near the Great Wall.

When her grandma, Năinai, sewed her a red silk hood for her kung fu performances, she loved it so much that she wore it everywhere.

People began to call her Little Red Riding Hood, or "Little Red."

One day, Little Red and her mother heard that Năinai was sick.

They gathered herbs and cooked a pungent soup. Then they baked a big, sweet rice cake.

Her mother put the soup and cake into a basket and said, "Take this to Nǎinai. Stay on the path and don't talk to strangers."

"Don't worry, Mommy." Little Red drew her sword and leaped into a flying back kick. "I'm a good kung fu fighter. I can protect myself!" She picked up the basket and ran out of the house.

Little Red stayed on the path and soon
saw her grandmother's house in the distance.
Suddenly, a dragon blocked her way.

"Where are you going, little girl?"
Dragon asked in a sweet voice.

"To my grandmother's," she answered.

"Where does she live?"

"There!" She pointed at a red house in the shadow of the Great Wall.

Dragon moved closer. "What's in your basket?"

"A rice cake and herbal soup for my sick grandma."

"Pee-yew! Is that awful smell coming from the soup?"
Dragon pinched his nose and stepped back.

"Yes, but it will help her get better," said Little Red.

"That smelly soup will only make her sicker!" laughed Dragon.
"You know what would make your grandma better?"

"Ginseng! My mother and I looked for it, but we couldn't
find any."

"Well! There is a big ginseng root under that old tree."
Dragon pointed to the forest.

"Oh, thank you! I must get it for my grandma!"
Little Red forgot what her mother had told her
and ran off the path.

Meanwhile, Dragon hurried to Nǎinai's
house and knocked on the door.

难 得 糊 涂

"Is that you, my Little Red Riding Hood?"

"Yes, Năinai," said Dragon in a high-pitched voice.

"Come in, my dear! I am too weak to get up."

Dragon burst into the house. Without a word,
he leaped over to Nǎinai and swallowed her whole.
Then he put on one of her nightgowns and caps
and slid under the bedcovers.

When Little Red reached Năinai's house, she was surprised to find the door half open.

"Năinai!" she called out.

"Who-o-o is it?" asked a hoarse voice.

"It's me, Little Red! I brought you something special."

"Oh, my dear! Come in, come in!"

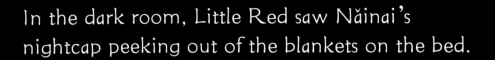

In the dark room, Little Red saw Năinai's
nightcap peeking out of the blankets on the bed.

"Năinai, what happened to your voice?"

"Oh, my dear, I'm sick with a sore throat."

"I dug a ginseng root
for you! It will help
you get better."

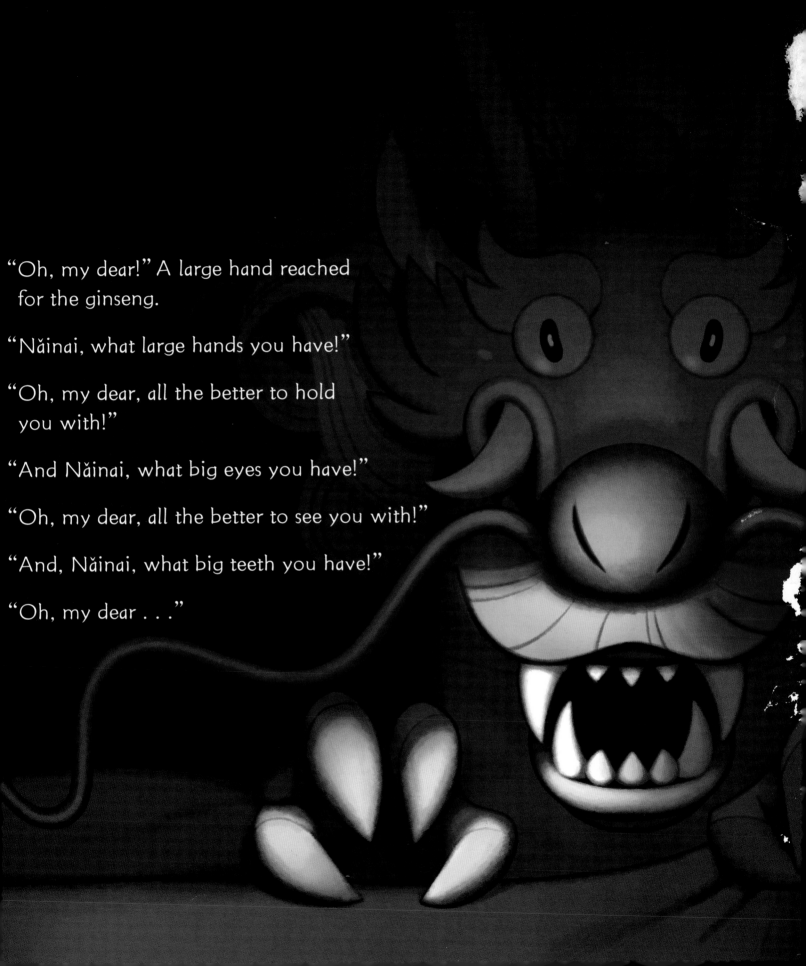

"Oh, my dear!" A large hand reached
    for the ginseng.

"Nǎinai, what large hands you have!"

"Oh, my dear, all the better to hold
    you with!"

"And Nǎinai, what big eyes you have!"

"Oh, my dear, all the better to see you with!"

"And, Nǎinai, what big teeth you have!"

"Oh, my dear . . ."

"ALL THE BETTER TO EAT YOU WITH!"

Dragon gobbled up Little Red and her basket and topped it off with the ginseng!

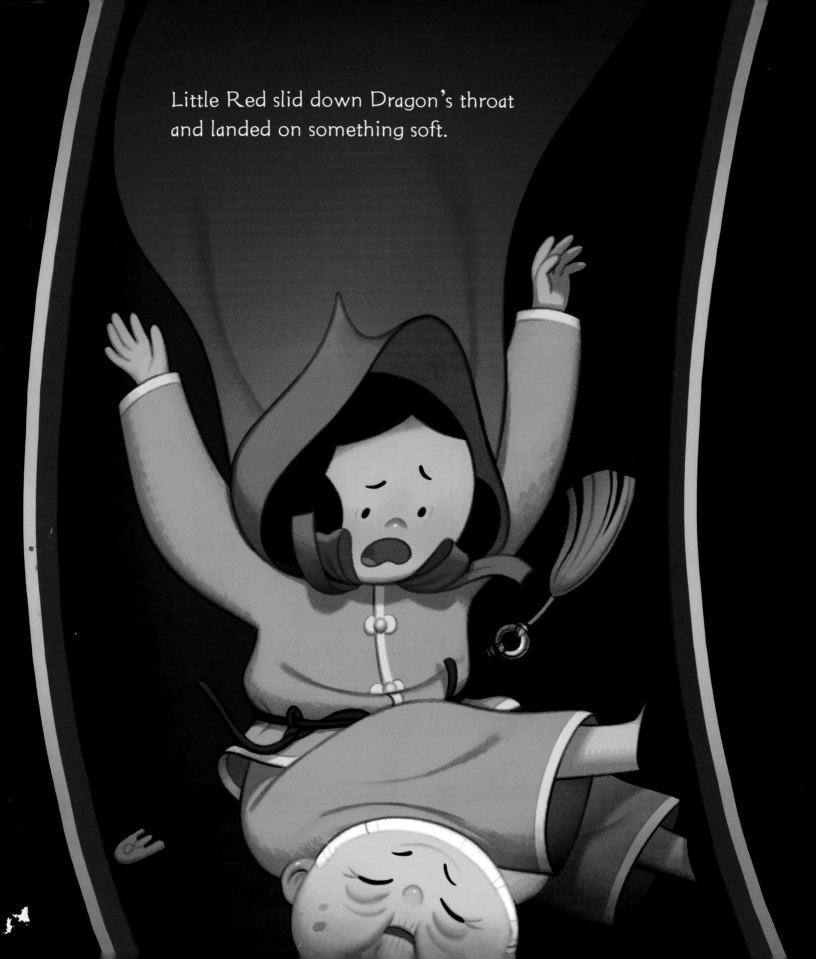

Little Red slid down Dragon's throat
and landed on something soft.

"Năinai!" shouted Little Red.

"Oh, no! He ate you, too!" cried Năinai.

"Don't cry, Năinai!" Little Red hugged her grandma.

"Look at everything he has gobbled up!"
Little Red rummaged through the piles
in Dragon's tummy.

"How will we get out of here?"
sobbed Nǎinai.

Little Red pulled a yo-yo from the heap, twirled it, and flung it high. The yo-yo bounced off of Dragon's stomach above her head.

Dragon yelped, eyes wide open in surprise.

Taking the ribbons in her hands, Little Red
spun around, drawing circles in the air.

The soft silk tickled Dragon's belly,
making him quiver and gasp for breath.

Little Red blew on a suona as hard as she could while Nǎinai pounded on a drum.

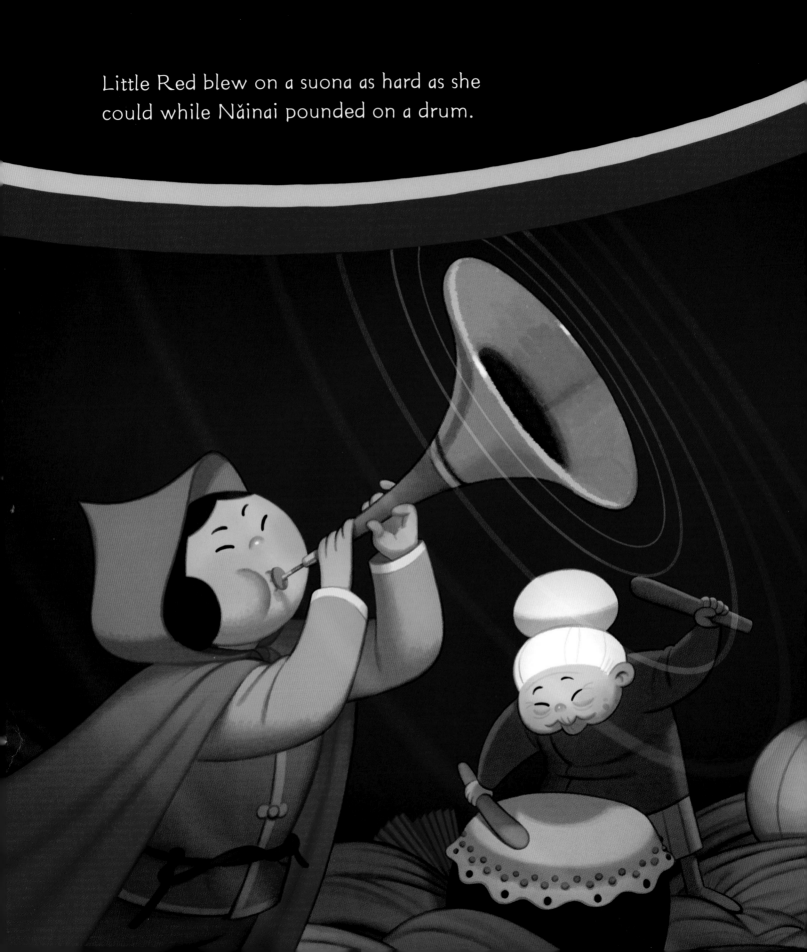

Dragon was so startled that he covered his ears and ran out of the house.

And then Little Red did her very best kung fu moves: axe kicks, crescent kicks, and roundhouse kicks. Dragon roared in pain.

Little Red splashed the herbal soup around.
Dragon's tummy churned like a wild sea.

He gagged and retched—then up came the soup, along with the yo-yo, ribbons, musical instruments, Năinai . . .

. . . and at last, Little Red Riding Hood, sword in hand.

Little Red jumped in front of Dragon and ordered, "SCRAM!"

And Dragon did.

To this day, Dragon stays far away
from girls in red capes.

I know because
I saw it firsthand.

Now that's the real story! I don't know how people ended up with a silly folktale that gave me, the gentle wolf, a bad reputation.

AUTHOR'S NOTE

Little Red Riding Hood is one of my favorite folktales. When I was little, I would have loved to have a cape like hers, as red is a lucky color in China. Like her, I also had a close relationship with my grandmother, Nǎinai, who helped raise me. For years, I wondered how the story would have ended if the woodsman had not come to the rescue. This question led me to write my version of the story—girls don't always need rescuing! I hope that my take on this folktale will empower those who read it and demonstrate that we can solve our own problems.

Chinese martial arts, also known as kung fu, consist of several hundred different fighting styles developed over centuries. Many Chinese children begin their study of martial arts at an early age to learn discipline and self-defense.

Kung fu words are very popular among girls who study martial arts. When I was young, my mother brought home a wooden training sword. For two years, I studied with one of our neighbors, an elderly doctor. Every morning, I would get up early to practice different kung fu sword moves before going to school. I was never that good, but it gave me a lot of confidence.

Dragons in Chinese mythology have many forms, but are often depicted as very large and snakelike with four legs. Dragons symbolize power and strength. The ancient Chinese even believed that solar eclipses were caused by a dragon gobbling up the sun.

Traditional Chinese medicine is based on thousands of years of medicinal practice. One of its key elements is treating patients with herbal soup. The soup can be very pungent. The Dragon's reaction to the medicine was inspired by my son. When he was young, whenever I cooked herbal soup, he would pinch his nose and threaten to throw up. (But he never did.)

Ginseng roots are believed to boost immunity and combat many diseases. The best wild ginseng roots resemble a human figure and are called ren shen or "root of person" in Chinese. In 2007, a Chinese buyer paid $400,000 for a 300-year-old ginseng root that weighed less than a pound!

I have visited different parts of the Great Wall. It is the longest wall in the world, stretching 13,171 miles from the western Gobi Desert and ending at the eastern Bohai Sea. It is also called the "Earth Dragon," or 地龙, because its undulating form resembles a dragon with its head dipping into the Bohai sea.

The Chinese letters above Nǎinai's bed read "Ignorance is bliss," a saying often found in Chinese homes.

WHAT LITTLE RED FOUND IN DRAGON'S BELLY

- Chinese yo-yo: made of two disks attached by an axle. It spins on strings that are pulled by two batons.

- Silk ribbons: used for martial arts dance. The performer waves two wands attached with long strips of silk to form captivating patterns in the air.

- Chinese drums: The pitch or tone produced depends on the size of the drum, the part being hit, and the strength of the player. They have been used in traditional and religious celebrations, and during warfare to command armies.

- Suona: a reed music instrument. It gives a loud and high-pitched sound. It's often used outdoors when people play folk music in northern China.

- Herbal soup: Traditional Chinese doctors use herbs to treat patients. The common way is to cook herbs in a clay pot with water to make a pungent soup. It often has a very bitter taste.

*To all the courageous girls around
the world that don't need rescuing!*
—Y.C.C.

To Kitty and Tian
—J.A.

The illustrations for this book were made digitally.

The interior font used in this book, Fāng Zhèng Kǎi Tǐ, originated from the "Chinese Standard KaiTi" script of the Shanghai Institute of Printing Technology in the 1940s. Its structure is well-proportioned and the strokes are round and soft with few changes in the thickness of horizontal and vertical lines. It is widely used in China in newspapers, magazines, and books, and commonly in textbooks. The cover typeface is an interpretation of Higumin, which was originally designed by Ryoko Nishizuka.

Cataloging-in-Publication Data has been applied for and
may be obtained from the Library of Congress.

ISBN 978-1-4197-3728-2

Text © 2022 Ying Chang Compestine
Illustrations © 2022 Joy Ang
Edited by Howard W. Reeves
Book design by Heather Kelly

Printed and bound in China
10 9 8 7 6 5 4 3 2 1

Abrams Books for Young Readers are available at special discounts when purchased
in quantity for premiums and promotions as well as fundraising or educational use.
Special editions can also be created to specification. For details, contact
specialsales@abramsbooks.com or the address below.

ABRAMS The Art of Books
195 Broadway, New York, NY 10007
abramsbooks.com